Button

WRITTEN BY
Andrew Torba
ILLUSTRATION BY DISCO

This  Book belongs to

_____

It was three days until
Christmas. Sarah wanted to be
outside playing with her friends,
but the weather was too bad.
The wind was blowing and the
snow was snowing.

Sarah's father knew his daughter loved playing outside. So, he decided to put aside his work and focus on something fun to cheer up his little girl. "Would you like to hear a story?"

Sarah thought this was a wonderful idea. Her father gave her a list of supplies for her to find. The list asked for construction paper, three popsicle sticks, some tape, and a button.

3

Sarah found the items on the list and brought them to her father. "What is the button for?" she asked. "We are going to make puppets," he said.

4

They laughed and laughed as they made them. When they finished, Father took the puppets and began telling a story. "Once upon a time, there was a kind woman. She lived alone in a big house."

One day she was looking at her garden through her window. She noticed a new family had moved into the  house across the way. The house had been empty for years and years.

There were not many children in the area. Day after day, she would see the boy in his yard all by himself. His mother was very busy with his new baby sister, and he was often alone.

The woman decided to introduce herself to the boy. She walked to her bookshelf and grabbed Button, a stuffed bear she had since she was a little girl, and marched across the street.

"Why does that bear have a button for a nose?" he asked. "This was my mother's teddy bear that she had given to me," she answered. "My mother said his old felt nose had been 'loved off,' so she had sewn a button in its place."

Each day, the woman and Button would visit the boy. Sometimes she would read him a Bible story. Or the funny pages from the paper. But she would always share stories of her many adventures with Button.

Then one day, the woman told the boy she was leaving. She was getting married. On Christmas Eve, the woman left. But before she went, she walked across the way and handed the boy a letter. He looked at it closely. It read "Open on Christmas."

Open on Christmas

It was time for bed, but Sarah wanted to hear the rest of the story. Father smiled. "It's time for the puppets to go to bed, too." He hugged his daughter, said a prayer, and kissed her goodnight.

The next morning, the wind was still blowing and the snow still snowing. Sarah was stuck inside another day. Only this time, she was glad because she wanted to hear more of the story.

She waited for her father to finish his work. She waited for him to finish his dinner. As soon as he sat in his chair, she approached him with the puppets. "What happened to the boy? What did the letter say?"

The boy woke up earlier than usual on Christmas Morning. He ran downstairs excitedly to see what presents awaited him under the tree. But instead of grabbing one of his presents, he opened the letter the woman had given him.

He smiled as he quietly read the note to himself. Then he dropped the letter and ran to the front door. He grabbed his lantern and walked into  the darkness. He walked across the way to the woman's house.

16

The boy hurried up the drive, looked around, and saw something on the walkway.
It was a present wrapped in the funny pages. A gift from the woman. He untied the bow and opened the box.

The boy giggled with delight. It was Button! His heart was filled with joy. He hugged the bear so tightly that he was afraid Button's button nose would pop off.

18

And the boy knew that he
would never be alone again.

19

Father placed the puppets down on the table. "Story time is over, Puppet, and it's time for bed. We've had a fun Christmas Eve," he said. He hugged his daughter, said a prayer, and kissed her goodnight.

As Sarah slipped into bed, she saw something on her pillow. It was a letter. It read, simply:

OPEN ME
CHRISTMAS
MORNING

It was Christmas Day. The sun was out. Sarah could hear her friends playing outside. She sat up in bed and opened the letter. It said, "Look under the tree, and you will find me."

Sarah hurried down the stairs. Under the tree, she found a present wrapped in the funny pages from the paper. She untied the bow and opened it.

Looking up at her from inside the box was Button. Beside Button was a very old letter. It said, 'Open on Christmas.'

"It was you.
You were the boy in
the story," she said.
Father smiled and
nodded.

25

He read her the letter. "I want you to remember that no matter where you go or what you do, you are never alone. Jesus is with you, in your heart, every step of the way. P.S. Someone is waiting to welcome you at my house."

26

Sarah's heart was filled with joy. She ran into her father's arms and hugged him tight.

And the boy knew that he would never be alone again.

The end.

Christ is King

Button
PUPPETS

*puppet images available for free
download at gab.com/GabBooks

Supplies list:
1. popsicle sticks
2. glue stick or tape
3. scissors

Giving and sharing God's love can transform lives and bring hope and comfort to those who are lonely or in need. The kind woman's selfless act of giving her cherished Button to the lonely boy, along with the time and wisdom she shared, highlights the power of giving to create meaningful connections and bring joy to others. The father's retelling of the story to his daughter emphasizes the importance of passing on the gift of God's love and the lessons learned from it. The letter and the gift of Button serve as reminders that giving is a reflection of God's love for us, and that by giving to others, we become vessels for His grace and compassion. Ultimately, this story teaches us that by giving of ourselves and sharing God's love with others, we can make a profound difference in their lives, just as God's gift of love and salvation has made a difference in ours.

About the author:

Andrew Torba is a Christian entrepreneur and best selling author from rural Pennsylvania. He and his wife Emily have three children.

The Gab Books Collection

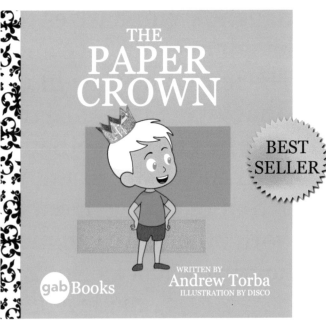

26421266R00024